CONTENTS

STAR WARS ™

THE CLONE WARS ™

Pedigree®

Published 2012.
Pedigree Books Limited, Beech Hill House, Walnut Gardens, Exeter, Devon EX4 4DH
www.pedigreebooks.com | books@pedigreegroup.co.uk

The Pedigree trademark, email and website addresses, are the sole and exclusive properties of
Pedigree Group Limited, used under licence in this publication.

£7.99

ALL TERRAIN TRANSPORT

Sometimes living transport is better than a machine. Tusken Raiders travel on banthas. The Nightsisters choose to ride rancors. What would you ride if you lived on a different planet?

Design a creature to carry you on its back. Don't forget to give it a name.

A IRON CAT That is BAt

NAME:

SUDOKU CHALLENGE

How long will it take you to solve this brain-teasing Sudoku puzzle?
Start thinking like a Jedi and engage your logic by working out which character should appear in each blank space. Carefully draw each one in place.

HOW TO DRAW
MOTHER TALZIN

Mother Talzin is the weird and wise head of the Nightsisters.
Follow these steps and learn how to draw this sinister sorceress.

1 Use lines and circles to create the rough Shape of Mother Talzin.

2 Add outline shape with light pencil lines.

3 Gradually add the some detail.

4 Complete your drawing with careful shading and sharp pencil lines.

Use this space to draw Mother Talzin.

MASSACRE

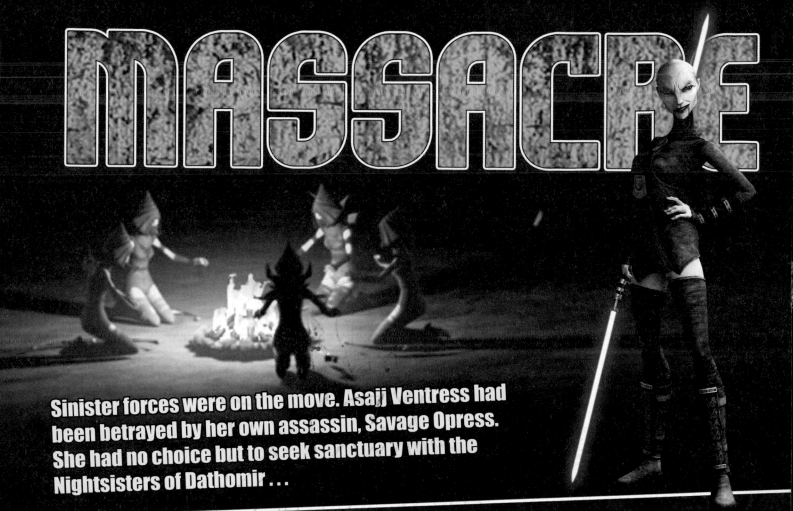

Sinister forces were on the move. Asajj Ventress had been betrayed by her own assassin, Savage Opress. She had no choice but to seek sanctuary with the Nightsisters of Dathomir . . .

Ventress landed her small Hutt fighter on Dathomir. She entered the Nightsisters' lair and found them sitting around a fire. Mother Talzin greeted her kindly. She could see that Ventress was angry and confused.

"Sister, I knew you'd return," she said.

"I've been hiding," Ventress replied. "Re-evaluating." Mother Talzin looked stern.

"You must give up the ways of the Sith and return to our fold," she said. "You will leave Dooku's absurd war behind and remain with us."

"And then?" asked Ventress. "And then you will fulfill your destiny and become a true Nightsister," replied Talzin. Ventress felt that she had little choice. Perhaps this was her destiny after all.

At his palace on Serenno, General Grievous was kneeling before Count Dooku, awaiting his orders.

"The time has come at last to take revenge on Asajj Ventress and the witch, Mother Talzin," said Dooku. "I have learned Ventress has returned to Dathomir. Go there and wipe the witches out. All of them."

"Yes, Master," Grievous replied, rising to his feet. He shouted instructions to his droid captains as he marched towards his ship.

In the Nightsisters' lair,
Ventress was led down to
a black, oily lake by a line
of chanting Sisters.
Ventress went down on
her knees.

"Do you pledge yourself to
the sisterhood? asked
Mother Talzin.

"I do," said Ventress.
"Do you abandon your old
life for this new one?" asked
Mother Talzin.

"I do," Ventress replied.
She repeated the words of the
pledge. Talzin submerged her in
the black liquid, and then used
magic to lift her high into the air.
Her old life was over. She was
reborn a sister of the night.

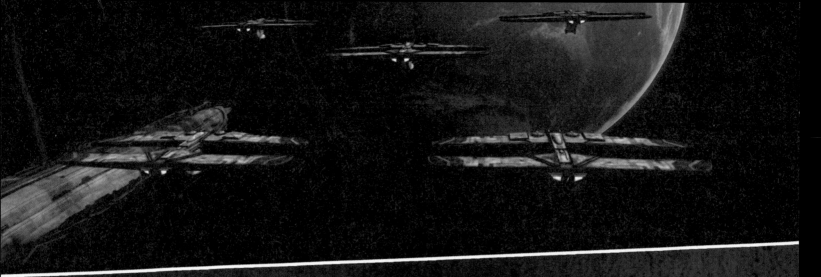

While the sisters were celebrating Ventress's baptism with a great feast, Grievous and his fleet were orbiting Dathomir. Ventress sensed that something was wrong. She looked up at the sky, and seconds later Grievous's fighters fired down on the Nightsisters.

"Droid fighters!" Ventress shouted to her sisters. "Scatter!"

"Prepare yourselves, sisters," cried Mother Talzin. "The war has come to Dathomir."

Grievous's droid army landed and began their assault on Dathomir. They marched towards the lair of the witches, burning their way through the forest. Meanwhile, the Nightsisters prepared to defend their planet. As they ran past, bows and swords in hand, Ventress started to feel afraid for her sisters. How many of them would die to protect her?

Suddenly, a pillar behind Mother Talzin and Ventress exploded and fell on top of Sister Karis. Ventress rushed to her side and used the Force to lift the pillar from her body, but she could not save her friend. Karis died in her arms.

Ventress was guilt-stricken, but there was no time to mourn. While Mother Talzin rose into the air in a mystical green bubble, blasting droids with her magic powers, Ventress ran into the forest, leading her sisters into battle against the droids.

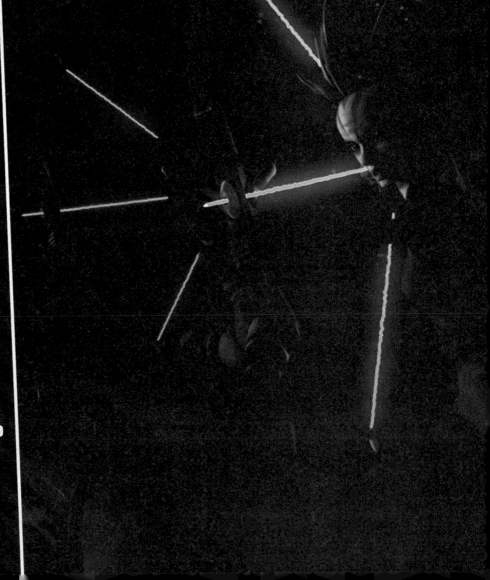

Deep in the forest, the Nightsisters were fighting for their lives. Ventress deflected laser fire with her lightsabers as her sisters attacked the droids with their energy bows. She led her sisters high into the treetops, where they attacked the droids from above. Slowly but surely, the tide began to turn. Back at the landing ship, General Grievous was fuming. He couldn't allow the Nightsisters to beat his army!

"Send in the defoliator tank," he commanded. "We'll burn those witches to the ground." The massive tank slowly lumbered into battle. As it wreaked havoc, Ventress and the Nightsisters were forced to retreat. They needed an army to fight Grievous's troops. There seemed to be no hope.

In the Nightsisters' lair, Mother Talzin asked two sisters to bring her a mysterious metallic sphere. She used her magic to reveal an opening that led her to a secret cave. There she found the oldest and wisest of the Nightsisters, Old Daka.

"I need you to resurrect our fallen sisters," said Talzin. "Ventress will need the aid of the undead army to achieve victory."

"Then I will begin the chant of Resurrection," replied Old Daka.

She shut her eyes and began to chant.

"Vlemon tagoo! Rise, rise, awake dead sisters, rise! Rise, rise, wake dead sisters, rise!"

As she spoke, a horde of undead Nightsisters appeared in the dark forest. They dropped from the trees like rotten fruit and raced towards the battlefield with a terrible wail.

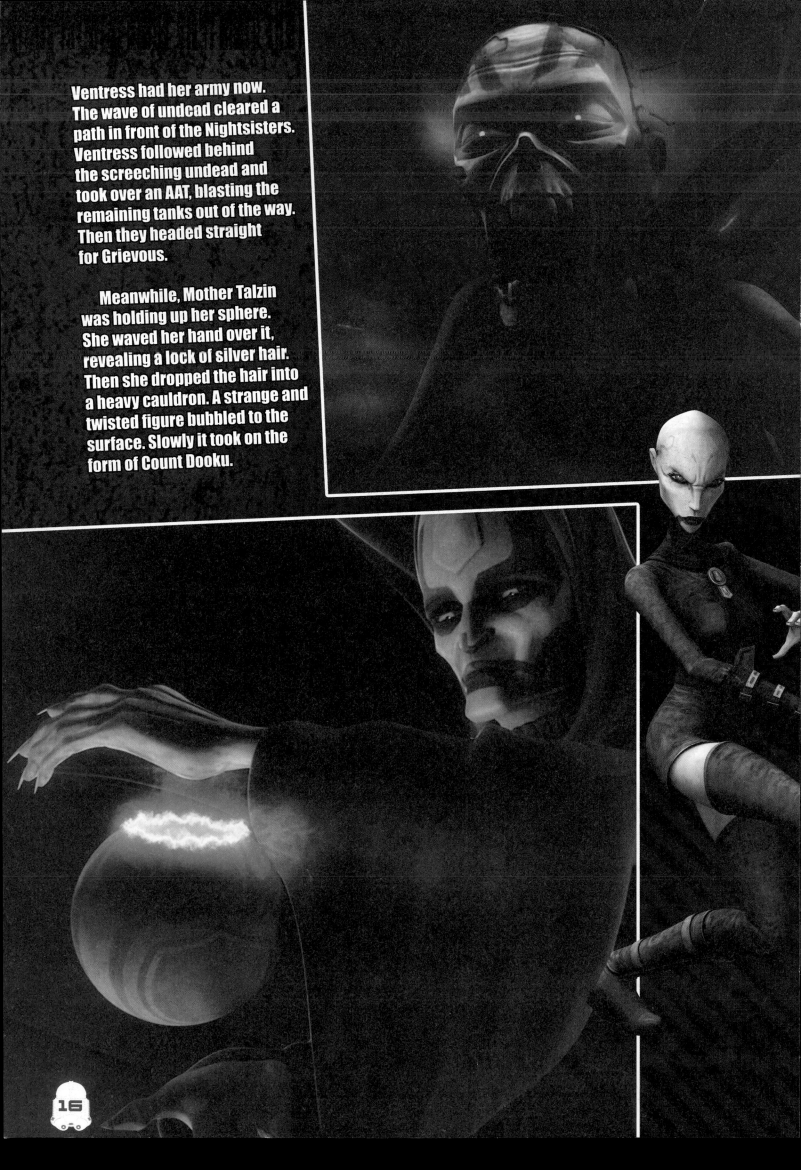

Ventress had her army now. The wave of undead cleared a path in front of the Nightsisters. Ventress followed behind the screeching undead and took over an AAT, blasting the remaining tanks out of the way. Then they headed straight for Grievous.

Meanwhile, Mother Talzin was holding up her sphere. She waved her hand over it, revealing a lock of silver hair. Then she dropped the hair into a heavy cauldron. A strange and twisted figure bubbled to the surface. Slowly it took on the form of Count Dooku.

On Serenno, Count Dooku was watching the attack via holograph. Suddenly, he gripped his face and fell to his knees, bellowing in pain. Shiny red boils magically erupted on his forehead. He knew that only one person could be responsible: Talzin!

Ventress arrived at Grievous's ship and faced the cyborg general.
"Fight me alone, prove you're the greater warrior," she demanded. "If I win, your army leaves. If you win, the Nightsisters will surrender to you."
Grievous smiled.
"I have always been greater than you," he shouted.

He swung his lightsaber and struck at Ventress. They fought with all their skill and strength and it was a fearsome duel, but at last Ventress gained the upper hand. With a lightning blow, she severed Grievous's arm. He staggered to his knees, ordering his droids to finish her.

Ventress was surrounded. But as the droids moved in on her, a wave of undead sisters swept into the clearing. Ventress slipped away into the forest.

Count Dooku continued to writhe in pain as Mother Talzin tormented him. He made a desperate call to Grievous, instructing him to stop Talzin at all costs.

After a mighty battle with the remaining undead, Grievous and his army followed a trail of green mist to the secret cave. The Nightsisters tried to protect their lair, but they were overwhelmed. A rocket exploded into the secret cave.

Grievous struck Old Daka to the ground and the remaining undead collapsed. The Nightsisters were defeated! Before she could be seized, Mother Talzin disappeared into green smoke. Her cauldron lay on its side, and Dooku was released from the spell.

Exhausted, Ventress ran deeper into the forest. Suddenly she saw a smoky, green vision of Mother Talzin. Ventress understood that the battle was over, and that her sisters had lost. She fell to her knees. None of her sisters remained – what was left for her now?

"This chapter is over," said the vision of Mother Talzin. "Your destiny will always be linked with ours, but you have your own path to follow now." The vision started to disappear again.

"No!" cried Ventress. "Wait! You can't leave me here!" She reached out to Mother Talzin, but there was nothing left but smoke.

Ventress was left alone in the deafening silence.

WHO'S WHO?

Look carefully at these burned fragments of photographs. They have been recovered from the massacre on Dathomir. Can you identify the people in the pictures?

1

COOL Mis

2

OBeonecAnoBe

3

DARK DRAK

4

BUILD AN ARMY

Grievous has arrived on Dathomir with his army.
But an accident has broken several of his droid soldiers!
Count up the number of heads and the number of bodies.
How many complete droids can you make?

ANSWER

22

HIRED KILLER

Bounty hunters are assassins for hire. The rich of the galaxy can pay them to do their dirty work.

Imagine that you are a powerful gangster like Jabba the Hutt. What sort of bounty hunter would you choose to hire? Use this space to design your perfect bounty hunter. Make a list of their skills and weapons, and give them a unique name.

Skills:
....
....
....
....
....
....
....

Weapons
....
....
....
....
....
....
....

NAME:

DARK SIDE DUEL

Use the grid to copy and colour this exciting picture of the duel between Asajj Ventress and General Grievous on Dathomir.

To fool the invading droid army, Mother Talzin has used her magic powers to create several versions of herself. But there is something different about the original Nightsister. Can you find the real Mother Talzin among the fakes?

BATTLE

STATISTICS

The clash of the Nightsisters and the droid army was an epic and chilling battle. Use this picture to record some of the battle statistics for history. Count the number of fighters, weapons and objects and fill in the boxes below.

AAT

Super Battle Droid

Commando Droid

Battle Droids

Energy Bows

Lightsabers

Living Nightsisters

Swords

Undead Nightsisters

BOUNTY

Asajj Ventress entered the Mos Eisley Cantina on Tatooine and ordered a drink. Since the massacre of the Nightsisters of Dathomir by Count Dooku's forces, she had been wandering through the Outer Rim. She was living among the castaways and vagabonds of the galaxy.

Ventress slammed the empty glass down as an alien called Oked spoke to her. Ventress ignored him. She was in no mood for small talk.

"Hey! I'm talkin' to you, lady," said the alien.

He grabbed her wrist. In one quick move, Ventress impaled him with her lightsaber. "I'm not much of a talker," she said.

A lizard at the back of the bar was staring at her. He beckoned her over.

"What do you want?" asked Ventress.

"I'm Bossk," said the lizard, "and this is Latts Razzi. We're bounty hunters, and . . ."

". . . we have a problem," finished Latts.

Ventress's hands went to her lightsabers, ready for a fight.

"You just killed one of our team," said Bossk.

"Sorry about that," said Ventress.

Bossk eyed her warily and she waited for the trouble to start. But Bossk's next words took her by surprise.

"We have a job to do and you owe us a man," he said. "Join our merry band of bounty hunters, or we turn you over to the authorities."

Ventress's eyes narrowed. "What do I have to do?" she asked.

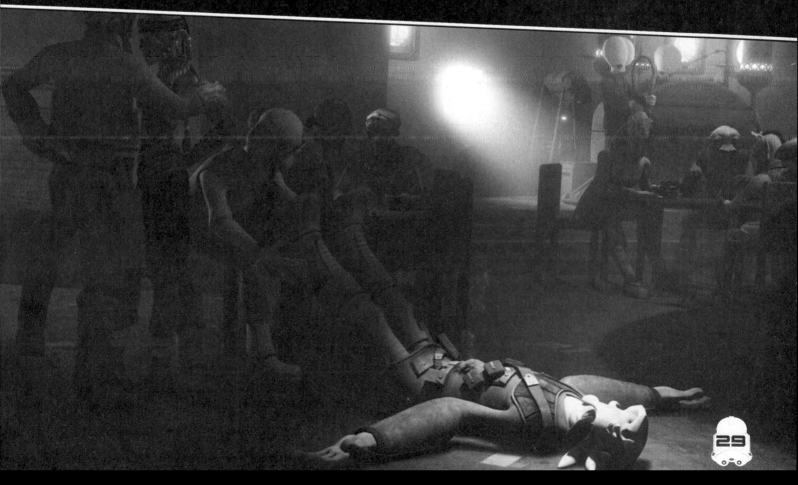

Ventress followed the bounty hunters through the ramshackle town. They were taking her to meet their boss. Inside a dingy room, a teenage boy was waiting for her.

"Boss?" she said. "This is your boss?"

"You got a problem with that?" the boy asked.

He introduced himself as Boba Fett. Ventress was not impressed. The bounty hunters explained that they need her to complete a job. She didn't trust this band of crooks, but she was a little short of work...

A short time later, the bounty hunters and Ventress left the Hound's Tooth, Bossk's ship, on a large space station orbiting Quarzite. Major Rigosso greeted them and explained their mission. They had to deliver a precious cargo to the Major's boss, Otua Blank. He ruled the planet with an iron fist, and losing the bounty would be the least of their problems if they failed to protect the cargo.

A large lift jetted them towards the interior of the planet, while Boba questioned the Major about the mission.

"Why hire six expensive bounty hunters to move cargo?" he asked.

"There's a group of marauders that would like nothing more than to hijack my master's cargo," said Rigosso. The lift came to a stop, and the bounty hunters saw a group of guards waiting with the cargo – a large, ornate box.

"No matter what happens, do not open this box," said Major Rigosso.

As the subtram pulled out of the station, a group of fierce Kage Warriors was hiding in the shadows. They were mounted on milodon.

"After them!" cried their leader.

The subtram whipped through an intricate network of enormous, crystal-studded caves. The bounty hunters were ready for a possible attack. Latts and Highsinger were standing guard next to the box.

Boba sent Ventress and Dengar to the rear of the subtram to secure the back platform.

As Ventress and Dengar stared into the tunnel, a group of shadowy warriors emerged from the darkness. Then two Kage Warriors leapt towards them and started to fight. Even more warriors sprang onto the subtram and surged towards the cargo hold.

Bossk and Boba looked up sharply as they heard the Kage Warriors running on top of their car. Rigosso began to panic. "They're here! Protect the cargo at all costs," he shouted. The Kage Warriors stormed through the subtram. The bounty hunters fought fiercely, but they were outnumbered. It

was all Latts could do to hold them off the cargo.

Dengar and Ventress were still fighting for their lives on the rear platform. Dengar was knocked over the railing of the subtram, and he watched helplessly as the subtram sped away.

Outside the cargo hold, the fighting was becoming more intense.

"Stop him, he's the leader!" shouted Rigosso. He pointed at Krismo, a skillful Kage Warrior. As Latts and Highsinger charged at him, he turned them against each other and threw them from the subtram. Now only Rigosso stood between him and the cargo hold.

"I want what's mine!" said Krismo.

"Over my dead body," Rigosso retorted. Without missing a beat, Krismo threw his sword into Rigosso, killing him instantly.

Krismo entered the cargo hold and kicked Boba out of his way. As the bounty hunter fell, he knocked the precious box open. Inside was a young girl, gasping for air.

Boba tried to help the girl up, but she slapped him hard. Krismo knocked Boba out with one kick. "Pluma, are you ok?" he asked.

"Brother, you came for me!" she cried.

As they hugged each other, Ventress entered the cargo hold.

"Stay back!" shouted Krismo. "That little girl is worth a lot of money to me," said Ventress. "Now step aside!"

Krismo and Ventress fought hand-to-hand. They were evenly matched, and eventually Ventress had to use the Force to subdue him. Boba climbed slowly to his feet while she tied up Krismo. Pluma watched her with contempt.

"I never asked to be ripped away from my home – my family," she said. "You'll never know what it's like."

There was a long, tense silence.

"I wish I didn't, but I do," said Ventress, quietly.

When the subtram pulled into the station, Otua Blank was waiting. Ventress dragged the box to the hulking warlord.

"Finally, my bride," he said. She held out her hand for her reward and a guard gave her a case of credits.

"Enjoy!" she called back over her shoulder.

The subtram left the station with Ventress on board as Otua bent down to the box, his eyes gleaming.

"My bride!" he gloated. "At last!"

He opened the box and then staggered backwards. Instead of Pluma, the box contained Boba Fett, bound and gagged!

Ventress held Pluma at lightsaber point as Krismo walked ahead. The subtram stopped in the middle of nowhere and Krismo whistled for his mount. It returned with a group of Kage Warriors carrying a pile of credits. One of them threw the credits to Ventress, and she weighed them in her hand. Then she switched off her lightsaber.

Back at the space station, Ventress regrouped with the other bounty hunters. They had all been badly beaten, and they stared at her dejectedly. She smirked and threw the case of Otua's credits at their feet.

"Here's the payment," she said. "I already subtracted my share. Boba's is in there too, make sure he gets it."

"Well,' said Latts, looking shocked. "You certainly turned out to be quite the member of the team."

"I'm not part of any team," Ventress replied. "Once I was just like you, but I'm not that person any more. Now I have a future."

WHAT'S MY NAME?

Read these statements carefully. Can you work out which shady characters they are describing? Draw lines to link the characters with the matching descriptions.

1. I AM A CORELLIAN MERCENARY AND I AM ALSO KNOWN AS 'PAYBACK'.

2. I AM A CYBORG AND I AM WELL-KNOWN FOR MY ABILITY TO SLAY JEDI. I KEEP THE LIGHTSABERS OF ALL MY VICTIMS.

3. I AM A SITH LORD AND I TRAINED DARTH MAUL.

4. I AM A TRANDOSHAN BOUNTY HUNTER.

5. I WAS ONCE A JEDI MASTER, BUT NOW I AM A SITH LORD.

6. MY FATHER WAS THE TEMPLATE FOR THE REPUBLIC'S CLONE ARMY.

1.

2.

3.

4.

5.

6.

MOS EISLEY MAZE

Asajj Ventress has arrived on Tatooine and joined a team of bounty hunters in Mos Eisley. Help her to find her way through the shanty town. Her new boss Boba Fett is waiting for her on the other side of the slum. Make sure that she doesn't bump into anyone on the way!

STAR WARS

THE CLONE WARS

QUIZ

It's time to test your memory!

How closely have you followed Asajj Ventress's journey across the galaxy? Answer these questions about her adventures so far, and challenge the power of your memory.

1. Who was the oldest of the Nightsisters?

2. Asajj Ventress was reborn as a Nightsister beside a black, oily _ _ _ _ .

3. Which of the Nightsisters was killed by a falling pillar?

4. What was the weapon of choice of the Nightsisters?

5. General Grievous used a D_ _ _ _ _ _ _ _ _ tank to attack Dathomir.

6. The Nightsisters used an army of the _ _ _ _ _ _ to fight the droid soldiers.

8. Mother Talzin's magic appeared as a _ _ _ _ _ -coloured mist.

7. Mother Talzin tortured _ _ _ _ _ _ _ _ _ _ by using a lock of his hair.

9. Who killed the oldest Nightsister?

10. In what vehicle did Asajj Ventress arrive on Dathomir?

PART-1

11. To which planet did Asajj Ventress go after the massacre on Dathomir?

14. How many bounty hunters did Major Rigosso hire?

17. Ventress was supposed to deliver a girl called _ _ _ _ _ to a warlord.

12. Which bounty hunter did Asajj Ventress kill in the Mos Eisley Cantina?

15. Which warlord did Major Rigosso serve?

18. Who was the boss of the bounty hunters that Asajj Ventress worked for?

19. Which bounty hunter was knocked over the railing of a tram?

13. On which planet did the bounty hunters meet Major Rigosso?

16. Name the Kage Warrior who killed Major Rigosso?

20. What sort of bomb was used on board the tram?

Make a note of your score and turn to page 76 to complete the final part of the test.

SPOT THE DIFFERENCE

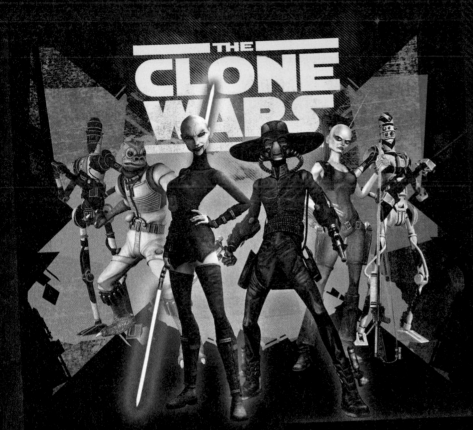

Look carefully at these two pictures of Asajj Ventress and her bounty hunter colleagues.

There are ten differences between them. Can you find them all?

CROSSWORD

How fast can you solve these clues? Each answer is connected with the adventures of Asajj Ventress.

Across

1. What was the name of Bossk's ship?
3. Who trained Asajj Ventress to use the Force?
5. Who used a metallic sphere to torture a Sith Lord?
8. What method of transport do people use to travel through the crystal-studded caves of Quarzite?
9. Who was turned into an assassin by Asajj Ventress, and then went on to betray her?
10. Another word to describe the Nightsisters is

_ _ _ _ _ _ .

Down

2. Name the home planet of the Nightsisters.
4. Which cyborg was sent to kill Asajj Ventress and the Nightsisters?
6. Who wanted to marry Pluma?
7. In which town did Asajj Ventress meet Bossk?

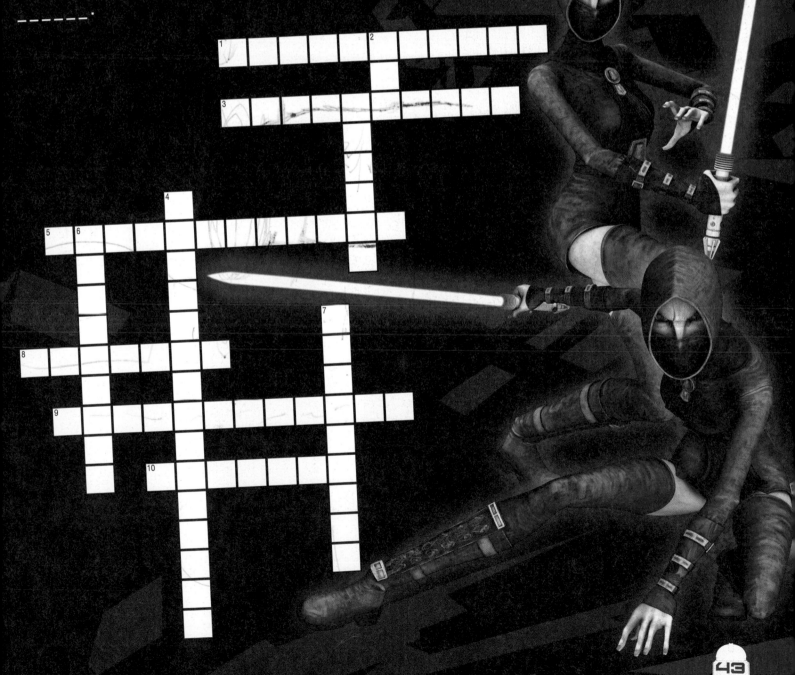

43

STARSHIP

Starship design is one of the most complicated jobs in the galaxy. Do you have what it takes to draw the plans for a super-fast new starship?

Use these basic blueprints to create your brand-new vessel. Don't forget to add the engine types, weapons systems and crew accommodation.

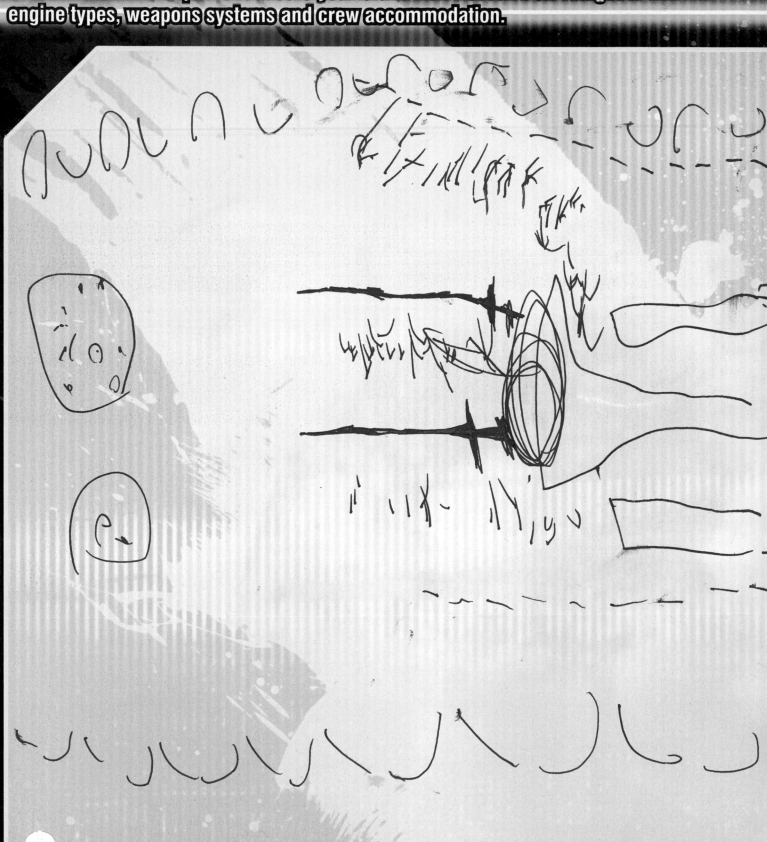

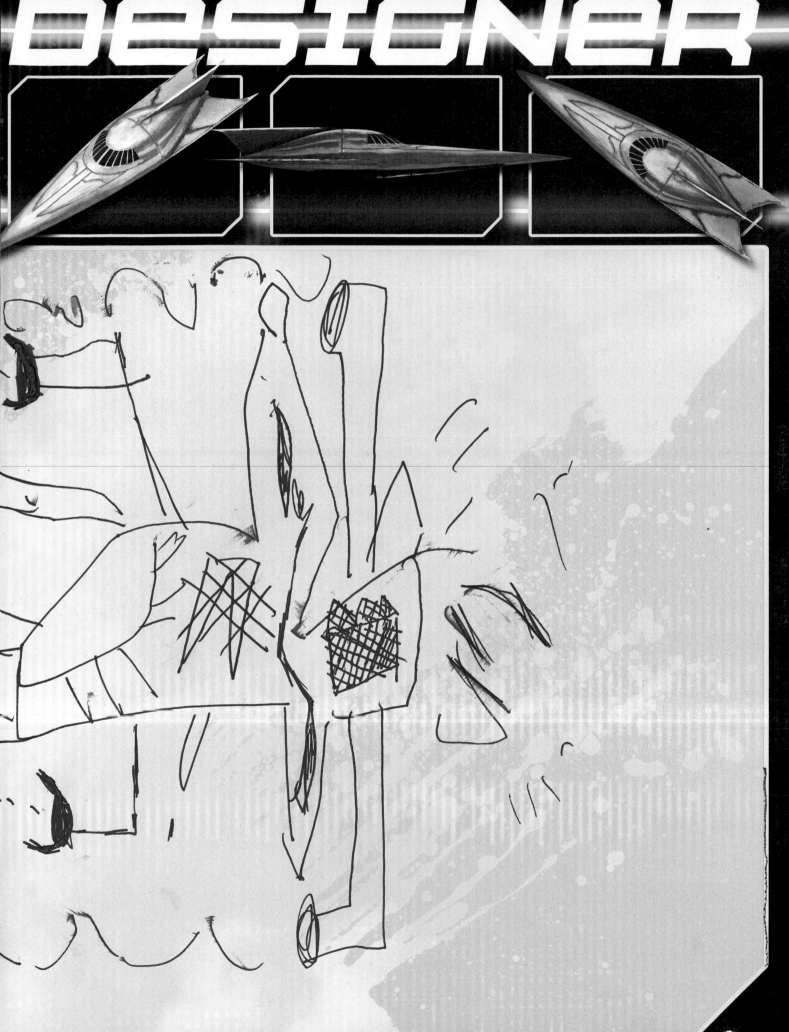

BROTHERS

Count Dooku's betrayal of his former apprentice, Asajj Ventress, resulted in the creation of a new menace in the galaxy: Savage Opress. He was caught in a deadly game of revenge between them, and he barely escaped the carnage. Beaten and alone, he returned to Mother Talzin, who gave him a new quest. It was time for him to pursue his long-lost brother ...

At a diner at Stobar Spaceport, Savage Opress was studying a navigation screen. He growled to himself. He couldn't find what he was looking for. At that moment, a waitress approached him,
   "What can I get you?" she asked.
   Savage barely heard her. The waitress noticed the golden talisman hanging around Savage's neck and reached out her hand.

Savage sprang to his feet and grabbed the poor waitress around the neck. The cook appeared from the kitchen with a blaster as the other diners panicked. Savage hurled the waitress at the cook and raced out. He hid between some dusty boxes, and at that moment his talisman began to glow. "This dust--it's a clue!" he said to himself.

On Dathomir, Mother Talzin was standing behind a cauldron fire. She was tracking Savage on a map of the galaxy that hung across the cave like a magic curtain.

"Yes, Savage, you are getting closer and closer," she murmured. "Soon you and your brother will be reunited."

Meanwhile, two Jedi starfighters were landing at the spaceport. Anakin Skywalker and his apprentice Ahsoka Tano headed for the diner. They pushed their way through the anxious crowd and found the local police questioning bystanders. There had clearly been some trouble.

As they waited for their food, Anakin tried to shake off a sudden uneasiness that had come over him.

"I sense a disturbance," he said. "Something sinister. Whatever it is, it feels familiar . . ."

Across the Galaxy, others could also sense the disturbance. On Tatooine, Asajj Ventress reached for her lightsaber as Savage appeared in her mind. On Serenno, Count Dooku paced up and down in his throne room.

"Savage Opress is growing stronger and stronger as each day passes," he said. General Grievous coughed.

"You consider him a threat?" he asked.

"He is a threat to all of us," said Dooku. "Even the Jedi."

Meanwhile, Savage had found the pilot of the ship that had carried the dust-covered boxes. He forced the pilot to fly back to the place where the boxes had come from. Soon he found himself on the junk fields of the planet Lotho Minor. His talisman was glowing brighter and brighter.

"I'm here at last, brother," he said.

Savage shielded himself from the harsh winds as he made his way through mountains of trash. A snake-like creature slithered by, unseen in the shadows. Suddenly, the talisman stopped glowing. Savage clenched his fists and growled in frustration.

"You trackin' somebody?" a voice asked from behind him. Savage moved quickly, stamping his foot down on the snake-like creature's tail and grabbing it by the throat.

"What do you know about it?" he demanded.

"I . . . I'm Morley," stammered the creature. "I . . . I could help you!"

Savage continued to squeeze.

"Trust me!" begged Morley. "Not everything on this planet is junk."

"Show me," said Savage.

A bizarre assortment of creatures lived in the junk fields. Some of these junkers devoured the junk, while others used the spare parts to modify their bodies. They were all alarmed at the sight of the trespassers, and they started to attack. But Savage drew his lightsaber and cut many of them down. The others soon retreated.

Just then, it started to rain. Everything around them began to sizzle and smoke.

"Acid rain," said Morley. "It'll melt us down if we don't find shelter soon."

They sprinted over to a hut as the rain began to pour.

Savage and Morley burst into the hut. It was lined with bones, old-fashioned weapons and corpses. Savage's talisman started to throb.

"This is it!" he exclaimed.

"It doesn't look like anyone's here, big guy," said Morley. Savage began to pace frantically up and down.

"Mother Talzin!" he growled. "She betrayed me! My brother must be dead!"

"She's not the only one who betrayed you!" shouted Morley. He slammed his tail down, and a trapdoor opened under Savage's feet. The Nightbrother tumbled into the darkness below.

Savage landed on all fours. Behind him, the shadows were moving.

"Brother?" he called out. "Is that you, brother?" His words echoed down the pitch-black tunnel. He ignited his lightsaber and started to move along the tunnel. Then he saw something move.

"Stop there!" he shouted. "What have you done with my brother? Answer me, you monster!" Then the creature attacked!

Savage lost his lightsaber in the fight and for a moment everything went dark. Then his talisman started to glow brighter and brighter. Its light washed over the face of the creature, and Savage gasped. It was Darth Maul!

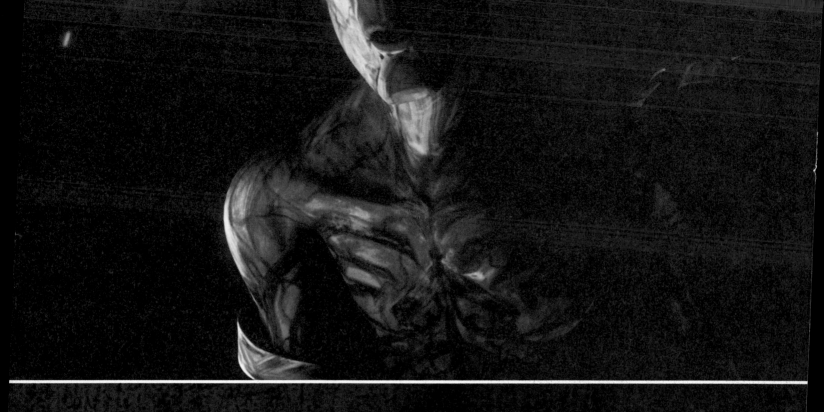

Maul retreated back into the darkness and Savage ran after him. The Sith apprentice's body was sitting on top of rusted spider-like legs. He started to rock back and forth, muttering to himself. Could this really be the brother that he had been searching for?

"You have been lost, my brother," said Savage. "Do you remember who you are?" Savage stared into his brother's eyes, looking for any sign of the fearsome Darth Maul of old. Maul stood tall on his spider legs and hauled Savage to his feet by his neck.

"Revenge," he said. "I must have revenge..."

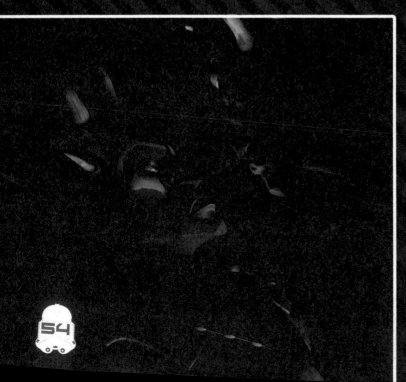

Far away in the Jedi Temple, Yoda was sitting in silent meditation. Obi-Wan Kenobi came in quietly.

"Feel the disturbance in the Force, do you?" asked Yoda, opening his eyes.

"Yes, Master," replied Obi-Wan. "Fear you are in danger, I do," continued the old Jedi. "From the dead, an old enemy has awakened seeking vengeance."

"An old enemy?" asked Obi-Wan.

"Killed your Master many moons ago, he did," Yoda replied.

Obi-Wan was shocked. "How can this be?" he asked. "I killed him myself!"

How could Darth Maul be alive?

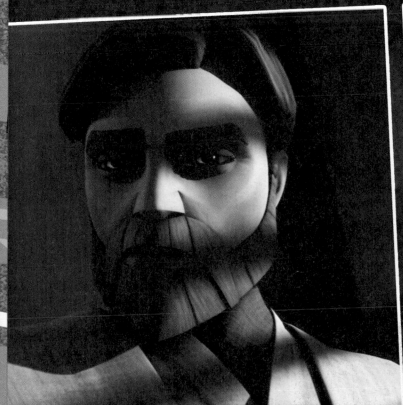

MASTER AND PADAWAN

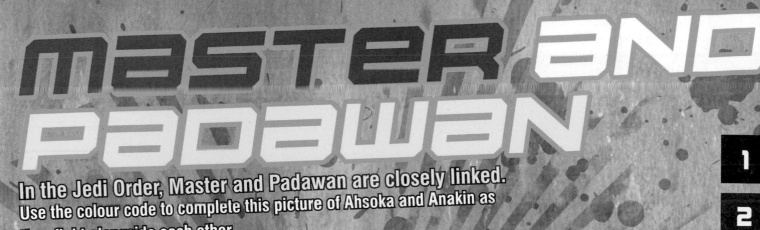

In the Jedi Order, Master and Padawan are closely linked.
Use the colour code to complete this picture of Ahsoka and Anakin as
they fight alongside each other.

THE CLONE WARS

50

SPOT THE SPY...

There are some enemies in disguise posing as Captain Rex. Can you identify all the spies?

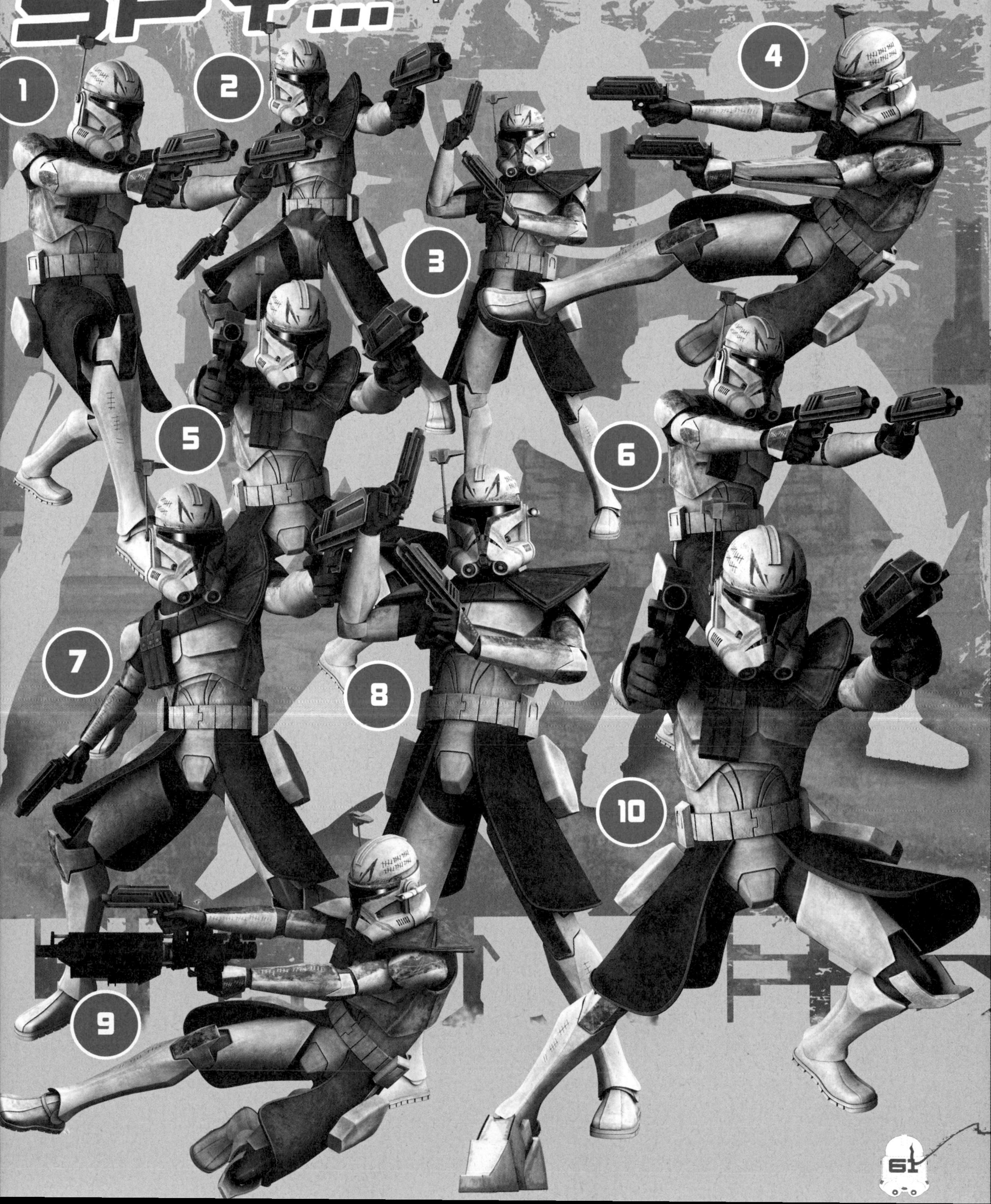

1

2

4

3

5

6

7

8

10

9

61

FRIENDS OF DEMOCRACY

These loyal members of the Republic are all defenders of democracy.
Use the Force and name each one if you can.

1.

2.

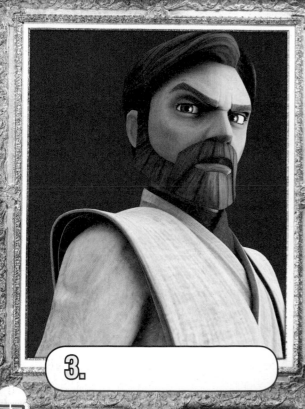

3.

4.

5.

6.

7.

8.

59

REVENGE

Everyone thought that Darth Maul, the Sith apprentice, had been killed years ago by Obi-Wan Kenobi. However, he was found alive by his brother, Savage Opress and taken back to Mother Talzin on Dathomir to be healed ...

Savage steered his ship through the dense fog of Dathomir. He looked over his shoulder at his crazed brother, who had folded himself tightly into a corner.

"Patience, brother," he said. "We're almost there."

Savage landed the ship and walked through the devastated camp of the Nightsisters, looking for Mother Talzin. He heard a voice, and then Mother Talzin materialised out of thin air. Savage knelt before her.

"Come, let us fix what has been broken," she said.

Inside her lair, Mother Talzin tapped Maul on the forehead and commanded him to sleep. She began to chant, and drew a circle of glittering green mist in the air above his head. Then she placed her hands on the sides of Maul's face and he screamed in pain as strings of black smoke were drawn from his head.

Savage watched as his brother writhed in pain and green mist formed around his body. A pair of mechanical legs took shape and become solid. Mother Talzin tapped Maul's forehead again and his eyes fluttered open.

"Arise, Maul, reborn son of Dathomir," she commanded.

"Brother?" Savage asked, anxiously.

Maul reached out his hands and held Savage's face.

"Brother," he replied.

Maul was whole again.

Maul's eyes were fierce as he tested his restored body.

"I was apprentice to the most powerful being in the galaxy once," he said. "I was destined to become so much more, but I was robbed of that destiny by the Jedi, by Obi-Wan Kenobi." His eyes flashed orange in the darkness.

"Then you must have your revenge, my brother," said Savage.

"Yes, we shall start with revenge," Maul replied. He began to make a plan.

Savage landed his ship on Raydonia, a small planet in the Outer Rim. Children from the settlement ran to the ship to greet the new visitors.

"Brother, what are we doing here?" asked Savage. "The Jedi won't be out this far in the galaxy."

"In a galaxy at war, Savage, there is only one way to get the attention of the Jedi," said Maul.

He ignited his lightsaber.

At the Jedi Temple, the Masters watched a holographic recording of the horrific massacre on Raydonia. Maul's message was clear. More innocent people would lose their lives unless Obi-Wan faced him. Obi-Wan closed his eyes.

"I have to go," he said.

"Not alone," said Mace Windu. "You see what he's capable of," said Obi-Wan. "He's a broken, unbalanced monster. I've dealt with him before. I can do it again."

Yoda turned to face the Council members.

"Against my better judgement, agree with Master Kenobi, I do," he said. "Finish what he started long ago, Obi-Wan must."

Obi-Wan left the chamber, and the other Council members exchanged worried glances. "Not alone will Kenobi be," Yoda continued. "An unexpected ally he may have. Trust the Force, we must."

A group of bounty hunters was gathered in the Mos Eisley Cantina on Tatooine, watching the local listings for outstanding bounties on a holo-transmitter.

"These marks are too easy," joked a Balnab bounty hunter. Then the face of Savage appeared.

Wanted: numerous murders, last known location: Raydonia, considered armed and very dangerous. Reward: 1,000,000 credits.

The crowd became rowdy and excited. Ventress downed her drink and climbed to her feet.

"Don't even consider it, boys," she said. "I've got this one." She downloaded the information from the screen onto her comlink and left quickly.

Obi-Wan arrived on Raydonia and walked through the rubble, stepping over the bodies that lay on the charred earth. Darth Maul was standing in front of a burning building.

"I have been waiting for you," he said.

"I'm not sure I've made your acquaintance," quipped Obi-Wan.

"I am surprised you could have forgotten me so easily after I killed your Master and you left me for dead on Naboo," Maul replied.

"I defeated you before and I can defeat you again," said Obi-Wan as he ignited his lightsaber. Maul laughed.

"Don't be so certain," he said. At that moment, Savage jumped out from behind Obi-Wan. They attacked Obi-Wan and soon overpowered him. Maul stood in triumph over Obi-Wan's body as he passed out.

While the brothers taunted Obi-Wan, Ventress crept aboard Savage's ship and hid. She watched Obi-Wan being beaten in the cargo hold.

"And they call you Master," Maul sneered, throwing him to the floor.

"When I cut you in half, I should have aimed for your neck instead," said Obi-Wan.

Maul lifted him to his feet, Force choking him, then ignited his lightsaber at Obi-Wan's throat.

"I will make sure you stay awake long enough to feel every single cut," he said.

Savage entered the cargo hold and immediately sensed the presence of Ventress.

"What a surprise," said Ventress.

Maul and Savage whipped around to face her.

"I was looking for a challenge, not some wretched cast-offs from the Nightbrothers clan," she said in a mocking tone. "What a disappointment." Before they could respond, she had disappeared..

Maul knocked out Obi-Wan, then he and Savage split up to search for Ventress. After they had gone, she appeared out of the shadows and shook Obi-Wan.

"It looks like I am here to rescue you," she said.

"When did you become the good guy?" Obi-Wan asked, struggling to his feet.
At that moment, Savage and Maul came back.

"The witch and the Jedi," said Savage.

"Here for our taking," Maul added.
He ignited his lightsaber, and Ventress handed one of her lightsabers to Obi-Wan.

"I want that back," she said.
"That's fine. Red's not my colour," he replied.

Obi-Wan and Ventress charged at the Nightbrothers and a vicious four-way lightsaber battle ensued. Maul taunted Obi-Wan by reminding him of how he had killed Qui-Gon Jinn. Obi-Wan's rage unbalanced him and Maul knocked him to the floor.

"We're outmatched," shouted Obi-Wan as he struggled to hold off Maul.

"You want to run?" Ventress asked.

Obi-Wan made his way to the cockpit door.

"Now!" he shouted.

Ventress flipped Savage away from her and Force-pushed him backwards. She jumped into the cockpit and shut the door. Maul and Savage stabbed their lightsabers through it.

"Hurry, Kenobi!" she shouted.

"Working on it!" replied Obi-Wan as he fiddled with the controls.

"Now would be a good time!" urged Ventress.

She watched helplessly as Maul and Savage began to cut through the door.

"Blast!" exclaimed Obi-Wan. He pounded the console and, just in time, the cockpit was ejected. The damaged cargo-hold door flew off into space, and the brothers braced themselves against the wall.

Maul hit a panel and a force-field covered the opening.
"What now, brother?" asked Savage, turning to Maul.
"We will be patient, Savage," he replied. "I've waited so many years for my revenge, I can wait a little longer."

Maul stared after the ejected cockpit as it flew away.
"But they will be coming for us," said Savage.
Maul turned to face him with a grim smile on his face.
"I am counting on it," he said.

TRUE OR FALSE

Can you recognise the truth among lies?
Read each of these statements about the last story carefully. Not all of them are correct.
Test your powers of insight and circle which are true and which are false.

1. Darth Maul was Asajj Ventress's brother.
TRUE / FALSE

2. Savage Opress took Darth Maul to Tatooine to meet Mother Talzin.
TRUE / FALSE

3. Twenty Nightsisters were waiting to greet Darth Maul.
TRUE / FALSE

4. Mother Talzin used magic to heal Darth Maul.
TRUE / FALSE

5. Darth Maul swore revenge on Anakin Skywalker.
TRUE / FALSE

6. The massacre on Raydonia was intended to draw Obi-Wan Kenobi to the planet.
TRUE / FALSE

8. Boba Fett rescued Obi-Wan from Savage Opress's ship.
TRUE / FALSE

7. Yoda foresaw that Obi-Wan would have an unexpected ally on Raydonia.
TRUE / FALSE

9. Obi-Wan fought Darth Maul with a red lightsaber.
TRUE / FALSE

10. Obi-Wan killed Mother Talzin.
TRUE / FALSE

THE CLONE CAPTAIN

DARTH MAUL MESSAGE

The Dark Side of the Force

Ahsoka Tano has stumbled across a message from Darth Maul. Can you help the young Jedi to unscramble the words and find out what the message says?

My Brother,

Once I was apprentice to Darth Sidious, and it was my destiny to rule the galaxy by his side. But Obi-Wan Kenobi stole my future and left me deformed and mad.

Now that I am whole again, I feel reborn. I will have revenge on the Jedi who almost killed me.

I will get his attention by the slaughter of innocents. Then I will make him suffer as I have suffered.

Vengeance is mine!

Darth Maul

CLUE: Looking in a reflective surface may help you!

STAR WARS
THE CLONE WARS

QUIZ

Time to test your memory again!

Your visual memory needs to be sharp and accurate. The second part of this quiz challenge is based on images. Look carefully at the pictures and answer the questions as quickly as you can.

1. Where was this picture taken?

2. Who wore this around his neck?

3. Who used this magical map?

4. Name this snake-like creature.

5. This character was known by two different names. What are they?

6. What sort of rain falls here?

8. Which Jedi Master did this crazed creature kill?

7. Whose legs are these?

9. Name this Jedi Master's home planet.

10. On which planet was this picture taken?

PART 2

11. Who attacked these people?

12. How much was the bounty on this Nightbrother?

13. In what vessel did these unlikely allies escape?

15. Name this group.

14. Name this planet.

16. Name the galactic conflict during which these Jedi met.

18. Who saved this Jedi Master from death on Raydonia?

17. What is the name of this old woman's clan?

19. Who was this Sith Lord's second apprentice?

20. On which planet was this picture taken?

Results:

40 – An outstanding result! You have a memory to rival that of a Jedi Master.

30-39 – Excellent work. Your powers of recall are formidable. Keep practising and your memory will only get stronger.

20-30 – You have done well, but you are capable of greater things. Pay more attention to the world around you.

0-10 – Your mind has been on other things, and this has let you down. Try to put your trust in the Force.

ANSWERS

PAGE 7 - NUMBER CHALLENGE

PAGE 20 - WHOS WHO
1. Asajj Ventress
2. Obi-Wan Kenobi
3. Savage Opress
4. General Grievous
5. Mother Talzin
6. Anakin Skywalker
7. Count Dooku
8. Ahsoka Tano

PAGE 21 - BUILD AN ARMY
complete droid soldiers = 16

PAGE 25 - TALZIN'S TRICKERY
No. 8

PAGES 26 - 27 BATTLE STATISTICS
AAT	= 4
Super Battle Droid	= 3
Commando Droid	= 7
Battle Droids	= 16
Energy Bows	= 4
Lightsabers	= 8
Living Nightsisters	= 15
Swords	= 5
Undead Nightsisters	= 6

PAGE 38 - WHAT'S MY NAME
1. e. Dengar
2. f. General Grievous
3. d. Darth Sidious
4. b. Bossk
5. c. Count Dooku
6. a. Boba Fett

PAGE 39 - MOS EISLEY MAZE

PAGES 40-41 - QUIZ PART 1
1. Uld Daka
2. Lake
3. Karis
4. Energy Bow
5. Defoliator
6. Undead
7. Count Dooku
8. Green
9. General Grievous
10. Hutt fighter
11. Tatooine
12. Oked
13. Quarzite
14. Six
15. Otua Blank
16. Krismo
17. Pluma
18. Boba Fett
19. Dengar
20. Smoke

PAGE 42 - SPOT THE DIFFERENCE

PAGE 43 - CROSSWORD

PAGE 56 - SHADOW MATCH
1. Anakin Skywalker, Jedi
2. Boba Fett, bounty hunter
3. Bossk, bounty hunter
4. Darth Maul, Sith
5. Darth Sidious, Sith
6. Dengar, bounty hunter
7. Latts Razzi, bounty hunter
8. Yoda, Jedi

PAGE 57 - WORDSEARCH

PAGE 61 - SPOT THE SPY
Numbers 2, 4, 5, 9 & 10 are spies

PAGES 62-63 - FRIENDS OF DEMOCRACY
1. Padmé Amidala
2. Bail Organa
3. Obi-Wan Kenobi
4. Ahsoka Tano
5. Ki-Adi-Mundi
6. Plo Koon
7. Jar Jar Binks
8. Mace Windu

PAGE 74 - TRUE OR FALSE
1. FALSE, 2. FALSE, 3. FALSE
4. TRUE, 5. FALSE, 6. TRUE, 7. TRUE
8. FALSE, 9. TRUE, 10. FALSE

PAGE 75 - MAUL MESSAGE

My Brother,

Once I was apprentice to Darth Sidious, and it was my destiny to rule the galaxy by his side. But Obi-Wan Kenobi stole my future and left me deformed and mad.

Now that I am whole again, I feel reborn. I will have revenge on the Jedi who almost killed me.

I will get his attention by the slaughter of innocents. Then I will make him suffer as I have suffered.

Vengeance is mine!

Darth Maul

PAGES 76-77 - QUIZ PART 2
1. A diner in Stobar Spaceport
2. Savage Opress
3. Mother Talzin
4. Morley
5. Count Dooku and Darth Tyranus
6. Acid rain
7. Darth Maul's legs
8. Qui-Gon Jinn
9. Stewjon
10. Coruscant
11. Darth Maul
12. 1,000,000 credits
13. The ejected cockpit of Savage Opress's ship
14. Dathomir
15. Jedi Council
16. The Clone Wars
17. The Nightsisters
18. Asajj Ventress
19. Count Dooku
20. Tatooine